Special Message

_____

_____

_____

_____

_____

_____

With Love, _____

Stick your favorite
picture here

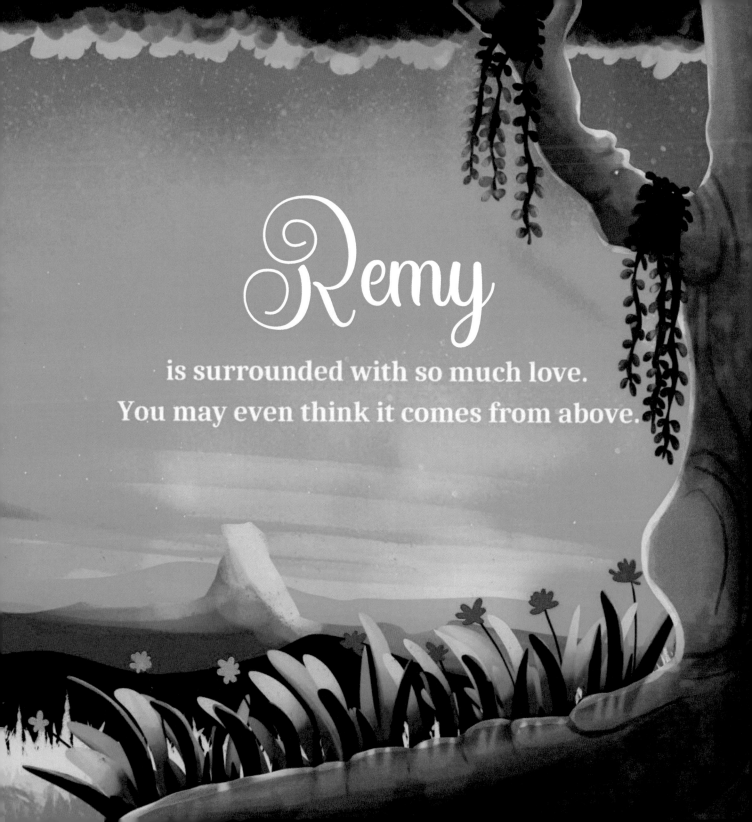

Remy

is surrounded with so much love.
You may even think it comes from above.

Remy

You are loved by the sky and the sun.

You deserve happiness and to have so much fun.

Remy

You are loved by the trees and the leaves that fall.
You are loved by everyone and all.

Remy

You are loved by the wind and the breeze.

You deserve the best hugging squeeze.

Remy

You are loved by the birds that tweet.

All because you are so gentle and sweet.

Remy

You are loved by the flowers
in the ground.
There is so much love all around.

Remy

You are loved by the moon and night.
You shine like the stars with the brightest light.

Remy

You are loved with your beautiful heart.
You are beautiful, amazing, and oh so smart.

Remy

You are love from your head to your toes.
You are loved by your family so close.

Merry Christmas.
Love, Grandma

Remy

You will be loved for the rest of your days.
You will be loved forever and always.

The end

Made in the USA
Las Vegas, NV
26 February 2024

86366632R00017